A Child Is Born

By Margaret Wise Brown

Illustrations by Floyd Cooper

JUMP AT THE SUN
HYPERION BOOKS FOR CHILDREN
NEW YORK

O come,
country shepherds
O follow the light

And welcome the baby
This blessed night

Come, wise men,
to worship
O come to the barn

The sweetest of babies
Is here safe and warm

O come, wild birds
Descend, gentle dove
And angels from Heaven
To give him your love

Come, little sheep
O look and see

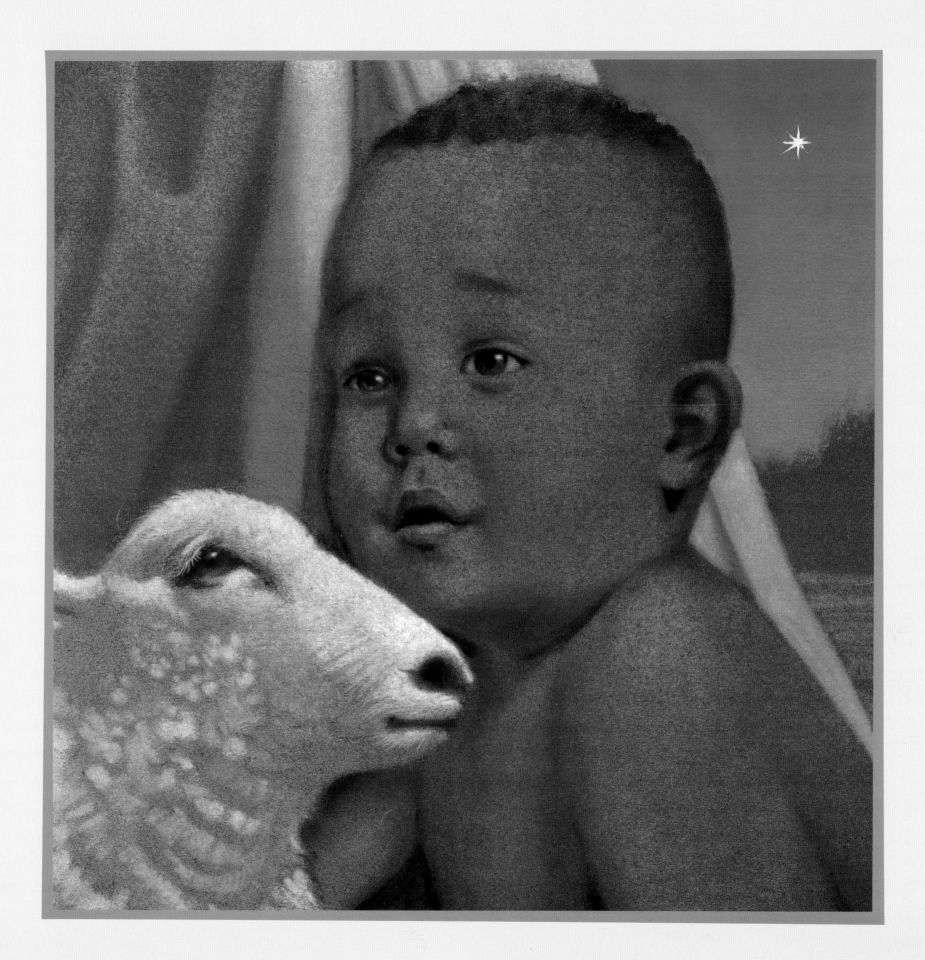

The baby is smiling
On his mother's knee

Come in joy, come in peace
O come right away

A child is born
On this Christmas Day

For Floyd Dickman, a true friend
~FC

All rights reserved. No part of this book may be reproduced or transmitted in any form or by any means, electronic or mechanical, including photocopying, recording, or by any information storage and retrieval system, without written permission from the publisher. For information address Hyperion Books for Children, 114 Fifth Avenue, New York, New York 10011-5690.
Visit www.jumpatthesun.com

First Edition
1 3 5 7 9 10 8 6 4 2
Printed in Hong Kong
ISBN 0-7868-0673-7 (trade)
ISBN 0-7868-2564-2 (lib. bdg.)
Library of Congress Cataloging Publication Data on file.